Dole

DINOSAUR
FARM

Other Teenage Mutant Ninja Turtles® books available in Yearling Books:

YEARLING BOOKS/YOUNG YEARLINGS/YEARLING CLASSICS are designed especially to entertain and enlighten young people. Patricia Reilly Giff, consultant to this series, received the bachelor's degree from Marymount College. She holds the master's degree in history from St. John's University, and a Professional Diploma in Reading from Hofstra University. She was a teacher and reading consultant for many years, and is the author of numerous books for young readers.

For a complete listing of all Yearling titles, write to
Dell Readers Service
P.O. Box 1045
South Holland, IL 60473.

TEENAGE MUTANT NINJA TURTLES

DINOSAUR FARM

D A V E   M O R R I S

Illustrated by Phil Jacobs

A YEARLING BOOK

Published by
Dell Publishing
a division of
Bantam Doubleday Dell Publishing Group, Inc.
666 Fifth Avenue
New York, New York 10103

This work was first published in Great Britain by Yearling Books,
Transworld Publishers Ltd.

ISBN: 0-440-40491-6

Printed in the United States of America

March 1991

10 9 8 7 6 5 4 3 2

OPM

HEROES IN A HALF SHELL

Fourteen years ago a group of four ordinary turtles that had dropped into the storm drains beneath New York were found by Splinter, a master of the skill of ninjutsu—the ancient Japanese art of stealth and espionage.

Then . . . a leakage of radioactive goo exposed Splinter and his pets to mutating chemicals. Splinter turned into a giant talking rat, while the turtles became the Teenage Mutant Ninja Turtles: his wacky, wisecracking, crime-fighting pupils.

With their human friend, April O'Neil, ace reporter on Channel 6 TV News, the Turtles fight for what's right and foil the nefarious schemes of the Shredder—Splinter's evil renegade student.

Meet Leonardo, the coolly efficient, sword-swinging team leader. Meet Donatello, the expert when it comes to machines; his swishing quarterstaff lays out his foes like skittles. Meet Raphael, the prankster, whose wry humor sees the team through perilous situations while his twin daggers send enemies fleeing in panic. And meet Michaelangelo, who's a master of the whirling nunchakus and is prepared to use them on anyone who gets between him and a pizza!

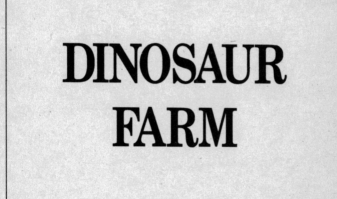

DINOSAUR
FARM

Donatello was enjoying his visit to the museum. He'd been having great fun wandering through the minerals exhibit, where he had seen a meteorite that was older than the Earth. After looking at a display of antiquated machines, he quickened his step. Now he was heading for the part of the museum he liked most of all—the dinosaur gallery. Donatello always saved the best till last.

Being the most studious of the four Turtles, Donatello sometimes liked to take time doing things that his brothers had little interest in. One of his hobbies was building and repairing machines—or sometimes just taking them apart to see how they worked. Another one of his interests was dinosaurs.

Of course, he had to make sure to avoid the crowds. Lots of people visited the museum every day. Many of them were children, more observant and inquisitive than adults and less likely just to file through the galleries taking a cursory look at each exhibit. In surroundings like that, even the standard Turtle disguise of trench coat and floppy hat might not have kept Donatello's identity a secret. And secrecy, as Master Splinter never tired of telling his adopted sons, had to be their watchword. That was why Donatello always made his visits to the museum at night.

This particular evening in November, the moon had just risen high enough to cast a beam of pale silver down through a skylight in the high roof of the gallery. Donatello stopped in awe as he entered. In front of him stood the bleached bones of a mighty *Tyrannosaurus rex,* the most ferocious flesh-eater in the history of the world.

It was only a fossil, of course, inert and harmless for the last 100 million years, but in the eerie silence of the darkened gallery Donatello could almost imagine what the tyrannosaur must have been like in life. As tall as a house and heavier than a truck, it had a mouth large enough to swallow a Mutant Turtle whole. His imagination filled in muscled flanks over the fossil skeleton and beady hawklike eyes in the empty sockets. . . .

Donatello suppressed a nervous gulp. *Maybe coming in here at night wasn't such a great idea,* he thought. *This place sure gives me the creeps sometimes.*

Suddenly a hollow clatter made him jump in surprise. Something was moving in the shadows at the far end of the gallery! Donatello instinctively ducked behind a tall display case even before he had time to entertain any fanciful thoughts about resurrected dinosaurs or the like. Peering out and squinting into the gloom, he soon saw that there was a much more normal explanation for the disturbance. More normal—and even less welcome. For there behind the mounted skeleton of the tyrannosaur, struggling to remove a bone from its tail, were the familiar figures of Bebop and Rocksteady, the Shredder's mutant henchmen. Behind them Donatello could make out the shadowy forms of at least three Foot Soldiers.

The tailbone was as long as a railroad tie, and despite their strength it took both miscreant mutants to lift it. They seemed to be trying to get it on a cart at the back of the room. Apparently neither of them had thought of moving the cart nearer, or of getting the Foot Soldiers to help them.

"Gee, Rocky," Bebop said suddenly. "I just had a thought."

They both paused and Rocksteady seemed to think about this for a moment. His rhino eyes blinked in the moonlight. "Duh, dat's interestin', 'Bop," he said after a while. They resumed their struggle with the heavy bone.

A few seconds passed, and then Bebop said, "Hey, I just had dat same thought again, Rocky."

Rocksteady gave a wheezing grunt and lowered his end of the bone to the floor. "Maybe you better tell me da thought, so it won't keep comin' back to bother youse."

Bebop put down his own end of the bone. He fingered his whiskery jaw and looked puzzled. "Dah . . . no, it's gone outta my head now."

It probably died of loneliness in there, mused Donatello. He glanced back the way he had come in to check if the Foot Soldiers were on guard. Another of Master Splinter's maxims came to mind: *The effective warrior is prudent as well as courageous.* ("Don't get in over your head" was Raphael's interpretation.) Personally Donatello would rather have charged in to stop the robbery, but on his own there was a chance they might overwhelm him with weight of numbers. Numbskulls like Bebop and Rocksteady might just have been stealing for the fun of it, but the presence of Foot Soldiers suggested that Krang and the Shredder were also involved. Donatello decided it would be better to get back and tell the others.

Using his skills as a stealthy ninja, he slipped silently around the edge of the gallery and eased a side window open. Just as he was about to clamber through, however, he had to make new plans. For at that moment, the museum's night watchman blundered onto the scene.

"Hey, what's going on here?" shouted the guard. He had been dozing behind his desk when the sound of voices had awakened him. Sleepily he fumbled for his gun while shining a flashlight along the gallery. The beam caught Bebop and Rocksteady. "What the—!" the watchman gasped, unable to believe his eyes at the strange sight.

As the guard froze, one of the Foot Soldiers sprang to action. With a blast from his laser pistol, he knocked the gun out of the watchman's hand. Another Foot Soldier closed in and threw the man to the floor with a judo move. They accomplished all this without a sound, in barely the blink of an eye.

Bebop swaggered over and looked down at the astonished guard. "What dis is, is a robbery, bozo," he said. "Ain'tcha never seen a robbery before?"

"Never by two guys in such ugly costumes," the guard replied. "Aren't you a few weeks late with the Halloween outfits, buddy? It'll be Thanksgiving in a couple of days!"

"Dese ain't no costumes, bozo," Bebop replied with a snarl.

"Nah, we're *naturally* dis ugly," Rocksteady added. "An' what you'll be in a few seconds is stone-cold dead, 'cause da boss wouldn't want us ta leave no witnesses." He drew a blaster pistol from his belt.

Donatello had been thinking a lot about Splinter's teachings that night. The most important of all, he knew, was that the Turtles would never abandon an innocent person in danger. He did not waste a second. Swinging his bo staff like a helicopter rotor, he ran forward and started knocking the villains down.

"Go on, run for it!" he shouted at the dazed guard.

The man looked up at him from the floor but showed no sign of moving. Rocksteady and Bebop, meanwhile, had shifted their sluggish brains into gear and were leveling their blaster pistols in Donatello's direction. The bo slashed out, sending the pistols flying off across the room.

"C'mon, dude, didn't you hear me?" demanded Donatello. "I can't hold off these lowlifes forever. Make tracks! Vamoose! Haul shell, pal!"

Rocksteady and Bebop took a quick look around for their pistols, but they had been knocked under a display case. Shoulder to shoulder, the two mutants charged at Donatello. Bracing himself, he set his bo out in front of him and met their charge head on. Slowly they began to push him back across the shiny marble floor.

"Haw, dis won't do ya no good, Turtle boy," Rocksteady chortled.

"Dere's two of us an' only one of youse. In case ya ain't countin', we got twice the muscle power."

"Yeah," agreed Donatello, suddenly sidestepping and whipping the bo aside, "but only half the *brain* power. . . ."

The two mutants had been putting their full weight into pushing Donatello back. Now, unable to regain their balance, they staggered forward with their arms flailing. Donatello swung the bo around to trip them, and the pair went crashing into the nearest display case. A

dinosaur bone, dislodged by the impact, rolled out and landed on Bebop's head.

"Looks like you're a *bone*head, 'Bop," Rocksteady said with uncharacteristic wit as his friend gave a grunt of pain. Seconds later a heavy fossil egg fell off the case and struck his own head.

"Haw, well, you sure ain't no *egg*-head," retorted Bebop.

Donatello knew that such a witless exchange could keep the mutants out of the fight for several seconds—but by this time the scattered Foot Soldiers were recovering. As they retrieved their weapons and began to close in, he again shouted to the guard to make a run for it.

The man sat up, but he still made no attempt to get away. Instead his face broke into a broad grin. "Hey, I know what it is," he announced. "You guys are students, right? This is some fraternity prank—kidnap a dinosaur or something. Sure, that's what it is. . . ."

Rocksteady had found his blaster pistol under the display case that Donatello had sent him careening into. Swinging around, he leveled the weapon straight at the guard's head. "Give it up, Turtle boy," he snapped. "Otherwise I'm gonna barbecue dis bozo's noggin."

"We'll turn him inta brain burgers!" Bebop chipped in.

By now the guard was beginning to get the picture. "Ulp . . . you're not students, are you?"

"Are you kidding, dude?" Donatello asked. "These guys never even got as far as learning to read!" He turned to Rocksteady. "Okay, I'll surrender—but first you have to let this man go."

Rocksteady got up slowly and prodded the guard toward the exit. "Yeah, sure. Who cares about him, anyways? It's you da boss is gonna be interested in, bozo."

With several weapons pointed at him, Donatello waited until the guard was safely away and then dropped his bo. "Shredder?" he asked.

"Nah," Bebop sniggered. "Da Shredder's on indefinite leave. We been pro-moted now—we're workin' directly for Krang himself."

Rocksteady pushed the muzzle of his pistol against Donatello's back. "An' we're takin' ya ta meet him. Move it, bozo!"

The Foot Soldiers ushered Donatello out a door at the back of the building. Rocksteady and Bebop followed with the cart—now laden with the dinosaur tailbone as well as various other pieces stolen from exhibits.

Donatello was taken to an alleyway where a strange vehicle stood waiting beside a mound of rubble. The vehicle was a large metal cylinder with a huge drill on one end and recessed portholes along the side. Rocksteady opened the hatch and prodded Donatello inside with the muzzle of his pistol.

"Hey, stop shoving, will you?" complained Donatello. As the vehicle's interior lights came on, he gazed around in awe. Intricate controls and flashing display panels filled the cockpit, giving a range of radar and sonar information. It was unlike any Earthly vehicle he had ever seen. But, with Krang involved, that was only to be expected.

"So is this supposed to get us to Dimension X?" he asked as Bebop tied him into a chair using the safety straps.

"We ain't goin' ta Dimension X," said Bebop. "Da Technodrome's on Earth now."

"It's under da Earth, as a matter of fact," Rocksteady put in before Donatello could register surprise. "A long way under. Dat's why we gotta use dese mole mobiles."

One of the Foot Soldiers went forward to the cockpit and began to flick a row of switches. There was the deep drone of powerful motors starting up and then, with a grinding of gears, the mole mobile tilted forward. A shuddering vibration spread through the vehicle, followed by a shrill whine as its drill bit cut into the concrete.

"Oh, boy, this is worse than a visit to the dentist," Donatello quipped at the sound. "And I'm beginning to get a sinking feeling."

Inexorably chewing the ground, the strange vehicle passed down and down through layers of rock. While joking to keep up his spirits, Donatello was actually keeping a close watch on the Foot Soldier at the controls. Donatello was a fast learner. Before too long he was fairly sure he could pilot a mole mobile, if the need arose. That might prove useful. . . .

"So, like, how far down are we going, dudes?" he said after a while.

"Oh, *miles*," said Bebop.

"Possibly farther," added Rocksteady.

Donatello studied a gauge that reminded him of a plane's altimeter, except that obviously it worked in reverse to show their depth *below* the surface. He was not familiar with the Dimension X units of distance, but he was able to make a rough estimate of how far they were going by timing the regular hum of the drill's rotation. Having seen the size of the drill bit when they had gotten in the mole mobile, Donatello knew how far each rotation would take them. When the pilot finally reduced power, he reckoned they had gone down more than two hundred miles!

When the hatch opened, Donatello saw that they were in a docking bay at the base of the massive Technodrome. For a person with his interest in gadgets, it was a sight to take the breath away. As he was taken past ranks of giant alien machines, he gaped in amazement at the thick cables that conducted power from central generators to all parts of the Technodrome.

"There's enough power here to light the whole of New York," he exclaimed with a gasp.

"More than enough," a shrill, wheezing voice replied.

Donatello whirled. Doors had slid open behind him, and a strange figure stood there. It was a tall robot with plastic skin, with unseeing eyes glittering from a blank-featured head. The midriff of the robot was cut away to form a control center that accommodated the bodiless brain that was Krang, warlord of Dimension X.

One of Krang's vestigial tentacles worked a control lever and the robot lumbered forward. "So, you have brought me a Turtle." The evil warlord gloated. "Well done, my hench-things!" Krang dissolved into gurgling and insane laughter.

"We got da bones for you too, Mista Krang," said Bebop, pointing to the cart that the Foot Soldiers were now unloading from the mole mobile. Most of the bones still had the museum labels attached to them.

"We'll only need the ones from *Tyrannosaurus rex*," Krang told the Foot Soldiers.

"An' we got a dinosaur egg," Rocksteady chimed in.

Krang rubbed his tentacles together and drooled eagerly. "*Egg*-cellent!" He chortled.

"*Egg*-regious, I'd say," Donatello grunted. "What kind of crazed plan have you got in mind now, Krang? Are you going to boil those bones for soup, or are you just planning to make a big wish?"

Krang gave a little shriek of pleasure. "Something much more nefarious, meddlesome mutant. Come with me and I'll show you."

Responding to its controls, Krang's robot body turned and shambled off along a metal-floored corridor. Donatello shrugged and followed behind. He had not given up thoughts of escape, but he decided it would be a good idea to find out a little of Krang's schemes first.

An elevator conveyed them to the master control room at the heart of the Technodrome. Row upon row of Foot Soldiers stood guard here under banks of screens that displayed various views of the Earth's surface. Some of the screens were overlaid with computer maps that showed weather patterns and the like, and some showed the deployment of missiles and weaponry throughout the world.

"Anyone ever tell you that you have a real megalomaniac's taste in decor?" Donatello asked.

Krang cackled in glee and waved a tentacle at the map screens. "One day all this will be mine!" he declared. "It warms my heart to be able to watch these screens and gloat in anticipation."

Donatello peeked through a reinforced porthole at the swirling subterranean magma outside the Technodrome. "I dunno . . ." he said dubiously. "You've got yourself in a real low-rent area here, you know. I mean, it's hardly the place to run the world from, now is it?"

"Not for long!" Krang vowed. "I intend to raise the Technodrome up to the surface. But that will take even more resources than I currently have available, since much of the Technodrome's power is spent keeping the red-hot rock outside from melting through. So I have formulated a plan that will make me overlord of the surface world. Then I will oversee my human subjects and have them raise the Technodrome to a preeminent position from where I can rule the Earth!"

"Well, it's an interest," Donatello conceded. "But don't you think a hobby like train-watching would be less antisocial? Or how about football? They could use you as the ball."

"Mock me if you wish, you annoying adolescent!" Krang cried shrilly. "I have conquered countless dimensions—your own petty planet will not hold out against me for long." He directed his robot arm to gesture at a gurgling vat in the center of the chamber. It was filled with a greenish-blue liquid that flowed sluggishly like molasses, and occasionally emitted bubbles of acrid gas. "Do you recognize this, troublesome Turtle?"

Donatello studied it for a moment. "It looks something like the mutagen that transformed Splinter and my brothers." He stepped closer for a look at the pipes that fed ingredients into the vat. One of them was discharging a substance that looked like powdered bone.

"Nearly right," said Krang. "You're bright for an Earthling."

"Believe me, I'm *really* bright compared to most turtles," said Donatello. "So, are we going to play twenty questions, or are you going to tell me about this brilliant scheme of yours?"

"This substance is a mutagenic virus that I have developed," replied Krang. "When administered to a creature, it causes it to revert to the form of its distant ancestors. If I gave a variant of it to

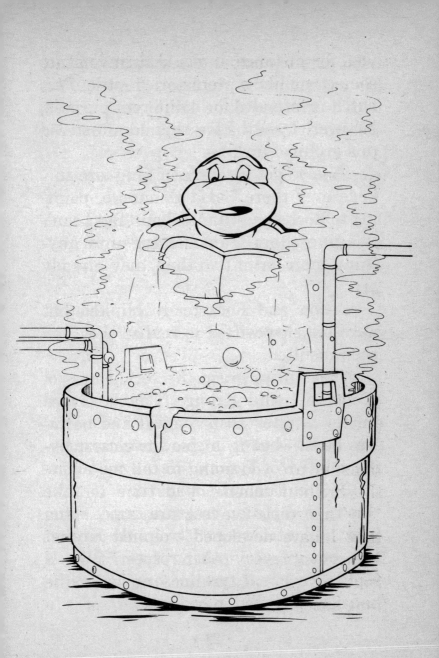

you, for instance, it would turn you into something like a prehistoric reptile. *This* batch is intended for a different purpose, however. I shall have this administered to a group of turkeys."

"You've got a couple of king-size turkeys over there," said Donatello, pointing to Rocksteady and Bebop. "But I can't imagine them transforming into anything more primitive than they already are."

Bebop and Rocksteady blinked but were too slow-witted to realize they had been insulted.

"You fail to grasp the seriousness of the plan," said Krang. "The farmyard turkey is after all a comical and harmless beast—but it is also the closest living relative of *Tyrannosaurus rex*!"

Before Donatello had time to take this in, a reptilian creature came loping into the control room. It was only two feet tall, but in every other respect it was a replica of a real tyrannosaur just as he had seen depicted in books.

"As you can see," said Krang, "I've already tested the virus on a turkey to make sure that it works. This is my prototype pet; I call him Tyro."

Tyro hissed at Bebop and Rocksteady, who were glowering at him with undisguised dislike. "Ya dumb beast!" Bebop said with a growl.

"Hey, dat ain't nice!" protested Rocksteady. "What did I do?"

"I was talkin' to da dinosaur, ya dummy," said Bebop. "Not you."

Tyro went over to Donatello and sniffed at him. To the Turtle's astonishment, the pet dinosaur then settled his fearsome muzzle into the palm of his hand. He was behaving for all the world like a dog seeking affection. Perhaps Donatello should not have been surprised; Krang and his lackeys were not the sort to give the animal any affection themselves.

"He seems to like you," said Krang. "Or maybe he wants to take a bite of Turtle."

"Obviously he doesn't much care for the company he's been keeping up to now," said Donatello. He knelt down and patted the miniature dinosaur. Then, on a whim, he took off his purple bandanna and slipped it around Tyro's neck. "Here you go, boy, here's a collar for you."

"He may seem docile enough now," hissed Krang, "but imagine if he were hungry. Imagine if there were thousands like him, all hungry. Actually, you won't have to imagine it—in a couple of days that'll be the scene on the streets of New York City. I've nearly got enough virus for one whole farm."

Donatello glared at him. "You're out of your skull, Krang." He looked from the robot's head to the control center in its abdomen. "Like *undeniably* out of your skull. Don't you think my brothers will get wise to your schemes when I don't return? They'll be on your tail in no time—if you had a tail, that is. You'll never get the chance to put your dastardly plan into effect."

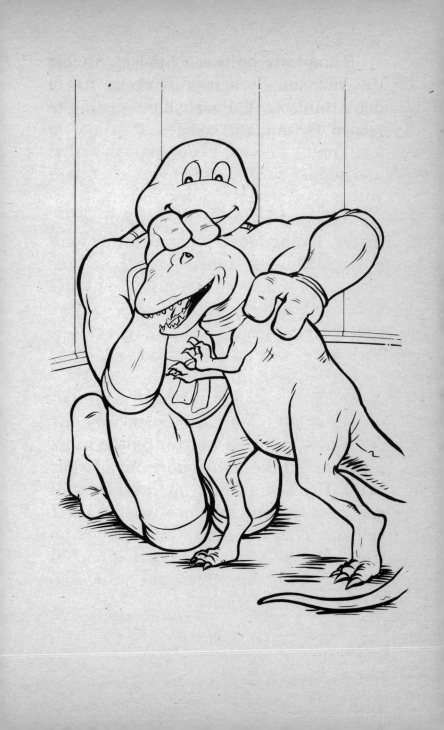

Krang directed his robot body to fold its arms smugly across its chest. "Oh, I don't think so. You see, you *are* going to return. Or so it will seem. . . ."

The three other Turtles—Leonardo, Raphael, and Michaelangelo—were back in their den in the storm drains, watching a late-night film while munching at a couple of home-delivery pizzas. After some early problems, the pizzeria had finally gotten comfortable with the idea of making deliveries to a manhole cover instead of to a normal address.

Master Splinter came in, having finished his Zen breathing exercises. "Is Donatello still not back?" he asked, raising one bristly eyebrow as he surveyed the scattered pizza boxes and half-chewed remains.

"No, Sensei," said Leonardo. "But he ought to be back any minute."

"He won't want to miss *Godzilla Versus the Robot*," added Michaelangelo, fastidiously removing the olives from his pizza slice and exchanging them for some of Raphael's peanut butter cups.

Splinter picked up the remote control and flicked to another channel. "I suggest that before entertaining yourselves, my pupils, you should watch the late-evening news. Remember that the Shredder is always preparing some new and perfidious ploy, and we may be the only ones capable of recognizing the distinctive stamp of his evil handiwork."

"In other words," said Raphael, groaning because he hated to miss the start of the film, "be alert."

"What's a 'lert'?" asked Michaelangelo, but the others shushed him when they saw the familiar face of their friend April on the screen.

She was talking to a rather baffled-looking man in watchman's gear. "I'm telling you, those robbers were like something out of a trick-or-treat party," the man was saying. "And all they were interested in was dinosaur bones. It's a whole new line in burglary, I'm telling you."

April turned to the camera. "There you have it. This is the first eyewitness account, but these bizarre robberies have been happening for the last few weeks at museums all across town. In each case, a large mound of dug-up rubble has been found in an alleyway nearby. Who are the culprits? And why are they interested only in fossils? Channel Six News will have these answers for you, as and when we learn them. This is April O'Neil, outside the Empire Museum."

The three Turtles sat up in unison.

"Hey, that's the place Don was going to, isn't it? asked Michaelangelo.

"The watchman's story certainly calls to mind that villainous duo, Bebop and Rocksteady," said Splinter. He could not disguise a tone of concern in his normally calm voice. "If they were accompanied by Foot Soldiers, Donatello may have been hard-pressed to deal with them."

At that moment there was a knock at the door. The tension that was building up in everyone's mind found sudden release as they all sprang into action. Leonardo took up a position behind the door, ready to lash out with the pommel of his katana. Raphael moved behind the sofa and drew back his arm, poised to hurl a sai dagger at any unwelcome intruder. Splinter himself took a handful of shuriken stars from his robe, then gestured for Michaelangelo to open the door.

Michaelangelo eased the door open. Then they saw his tense posture relax, and he flung it wide. "Don!" he exclaimed. "You scared the living daylights

out of us. We thought Bebop and Rock-steady had abducted you or something."

"No . . . I'm all right . . . Michaelangelo," said the figure at the door.

"Well, what're you hanging around out there for, Don?" Raphael asked, sheathing his sai. "You'd better come and get some pizza while there's still a slice to be had."

"Thank you . . . Raphael," said the figure, stepping inside. Certainly it *looked* like Donatello.

Splinter's trained ninja senses were troubled by something. His whiskers twitched as he asked, "Is something wrong, Donatello?"

"Nothing . . . Master." The figure gave a shake of the head. "There is no cause for concern."

"No cause for concern, he says!" exclaimed Raphael, flicking back to the film. "We already missed the bit where Godzilla comes up out of the sea." He settled down on the sofa. "Look, there's the robot—"

"A robot!" Donatello exclaimed with a snarl. "You unspeakably devious fiend, Krang!"

"Why, thank you," said Krang. "It's always cheering to receive an unexpected compliment."

It was several hours after Donatello had been brought to the Technodrome. He had been wondering how Krang could possibly prevent the other Turtles from worrying about his disappearance. Now, seeing the scene in the den on a display screen in the control room, he understood.

"This screen relays pictures from video cameras in the robot's eyes," said Krang, grinning toothily. He was beside himself with admiration at his own warped genius. "Unfortunately I didn't have time to wire it for sound also."

"That's okay," said Donatello, patting Tyro's head. "I've seen all the Godzilla films before anyway."

"Still you mock me!" Krang declared, his evil little eyes sparkling with amusement. "Don't you understand, you vexatious crossbreed, that my plan is working? Your brothers believe you are safe with them, and there is no one to prevent me from infecting the city's turkey farms with a virus that will turn them into ravening carnivores."

'Haw, haw," Bebop chortled. "An' wid Thanksgivin' less than a week away too."

"I'd like ta see da joker dat tries ta put cranberry sauce on *dem* turkeys," Rocksteady put in, and the two moronic mutants laughed so much that they had to hold on to one another to stand up.

"Laugh all you want, dudes," said Donatello. "Once the others get wise to that robot, they're going to find their way down here and kick you from one end of this dome to the other."

He started to stalk out of the control room. Immediately four of the Foot Soldiers on sentry duty detached themselves from the main group and fell into step around him.

"We wouldn't want ya gettin' lost now, would we, Turtle boy?" jibed Rocksteady. Suddenly he gave a yelp of pain and started to jump around the room holding the seat of his pants. Tyro had crept up behind him while he was taunting Donatello and given him a painful bite. "Why, ya blasted brainless animal!" he yelled as the pain started to subside.

"Ya got no call ta insult me like dat, Rocky," said Bebop.

"Da dinosaur! Da durned dinosaur! It just took a chunk outta my behind, 'Bop."

Bebop glared at Tyro. "So it did, the little devil!" he exclaimed. "Well, I'll be a monkey's uncle . . ."

"What monkey would be stupid enough to accept an offer like that?" Donatello asked.

Bebop lunged at Tyro. "C'mere, critter. Maybe ya ain't no turkey now ya been mutated, but dat don't mean we can't spit-roast ya just da same."

Tyro dodged aside, leaving Bebop to hurtle headlong into the wall. Evading an equally clumsy lunge by Rocksteady, he loped off across the control room and ducked into an open ventilation panel. The two enraged mutants raced over in pursuit, but they were too large to fit through the panel. As they stamped their feet in frustration, Tyro gave a triumphant honking cry and then headed off along the ventilation shaft.

"Outwitted by a mutant turkey, huh?" Donatello remarked as the Foot Soldiers led him away. "Somehow I don't think it's worth you guys applying for membership in Mensa."

The two crestfallen mutants appealed to their master. "Mista Krang, it ain't fair," said Bebop. "Dat dinky dinosaur bit Rocky. He might *catch* somet'ing."

"I don't think so," said Krang. "Rocksteady doesn't have any infectious diseases, does he?"

"But *I* might catch somet'ing offa da

dinosaur," Rocksteady elaborated. "What about rabies?"

Krang was running out of patience. "It's a mutated turkey, you numbskull, not a dog! Now, go and visit the final museum on the list. I need another cartload of dinosaur bones to complete my batch of mutagen virus."

The villainous pair obediently shuffled off toward the docking bays. As they left the control room, Krang called after them. "Bring me a good consignment of fossils, my faithful but freakish minions, and I'll let you dine on dinosaur steaks when you get back."

That cheered them up. Whistling happily, they swaggered away to do their master's bidding.

4

But Tyro had no intention of winding up on anyone's dinner plate. Contrary to most people's beliefs, tyrannosaurs were not the pea-brained creatures many assumed them to be. Tyro was just about as intelligent as a pet dog—which put him on about the level of Bebop and Rocksteady, probably—and he knew enough to tell who was his friend and who was not. He could remember little of his former life as a turkey, but since being transmuted by Krang's experimental virus he knew that he had been treated as an object of scorn and cruelty. He disliked Krang, who smelled of ammonia and wet squid, and he positively *hated* Rocksteady and Bebop. The mutant pair had lost no opportunity to mistreat him, often delivering a brutal kick or at least a snide remark along with his food bowl each day. Tyro did not understand their words, of course, but he recognized the spite in their tone. Today, with all the preparations for robbing the museum, Rocksteady had forgotten to feed him at all. That was why he had taken a bite out of his rump. It was just a tyrannosaur's way of saying "I'm hungry."

On the other hand, Tyro had taken an instant shine to Donatello. He could tell that the Turtle was an enemy of Krang and his henchmen. More importantly, Donatello was the only one to have shown him any kindness during his short life. He had even given him a collar. Tyro stretched his scaly neck proudly, craning his head to admire the bright purple fabric.

He was crouching just inside a ventilation panel that looked out over the docking bay. Rocksteady and Bebop were loading the cart aboard one of the mole mobiles. Tyro's transformation had given him a hunter's instincts. He waited until their attention was elsewhere, then darted across and hid himself behind the cart in the mole mobile's storage compartment.

After a time, Bebop came back and sealed the compartment. Tyro heard the main hatch slam and lock, and then the drone of the engine as a pilot soldier gunned the vehicle into life.

Time passed. In darkness, with only the continuous thundering of chewed-up rock vibrating past the fuselage, he squatted down on his belly. It was a stance common to both turkeys and their distant saurian relatives.

Finally the vehicle shuddered and came to a halt. There was the sound of the occupants disembarking. With a clank, the compartment door opened. Tyro sniffed cool night air. Bebop reached in to pull out the cart. Abruptly Tyro leapt up from his hiding place and darted between the startled man-boar's legs.

"Dat dratted dinosaur!" Bebop shouted.

"Don't keep on about it, 'Bop," said Rocksteady, who was marshaling the Foot Soldiers on the other side of the vehicle. "We'll have it for breakfast when we get back."

"No, we won't! It's here now. Or it *was*—now it's gettin' away!" Bebop watched, too slow to react, as Tyro shot along the alleyway where they'd sur-faced. He vanished around a corner.

Hearing the enraged mutants giving chase, Tyro charged off across the de-serted street. The mutants drew their pistols and, seconds later, laser blasts shot just inches over his head. Tyro began to zigzag. He needed to find a place to hide where his ponderous tormentors could not follow. Then he spied just the thing—a large open hole in the ground.

It was in a section of road that was being repaired. Tyro slipped under the cordon the workmen had left around it and dropped through into the darkness of the storm drains.

◆

Down in the Turtles' den, Master Splinter was unable to sleep. He had been worried by Donatello's strange behavior since returning home that evening. There was nothing he could quite put his finger on, but Donatello certainly seemed distracted about something. The connection with the museum heists was too much to be a mere coincidence.

Splinter went and woke the Turtles. "Rise and shine, my sons," he said. "It is time for practice."

Michaelangelo yawned and tried to stuff his head back under the covers. But when Leonardo tipped Mike's mattress over, he realized he couldn't get away with pretending to be still asleep. "We might be able to rise, Master, but it's a tall order asking us to shine as well."

"Too true," agreed Raphael, crawling blearily from under his quilt. "Are we going out as early birds to catch worms, or what?"

"I am surprised at you, my students," Splinter said with a smile. "Why, at your age I would regularly get up before dawn for an hour or two of exercise."

Even Leonardo, dedicated as he was, was still unhappily rubbing the sleep from his eyes. "But maybe Dawn didn't get up so early in those days, Master," he said.

"Yeah, like it was nearly a hundred years ago *at least*," Raphael mumbled under his breath as he staggered over to the sink.

"Thank *you*, Raphael. I am not quite

that old," said Splinter, catching the remark with his extra-sharp hearing. "And
what about you, Donatello? No com-
plaints?"

"No . . . Master. Thank you for waking
me," said the robot Donatello.

Splinter stroked his whiskers, his
smile fading. Donatello was behaving in
a very worrisome manner. Still trying to
puzzle this out, Splinter watched the
Turtles gather around the breakfast table. Breakfast, as usual, was the cold
remains of yesterday's pizzas.

"Yum!" Michaelangelo said. "I swear,
dudes, I don't know if a pizza's tastier
when it's hot or when it's cold."

"How would you know, Mike?" Raphael asked grumpily. "It goes over your
tongue and down into your stomach too
fast for you to taste it."

Leonardo munched at his own slice
and then turned to "Donatello." "Hey,
Don, I think we must have gotten the
slices with all the anchovies—"

He broke off and stared in surprise.

Even though all the Turtles disliked anchovies, the robot Donatello was devouring his own pizza slice without a murmur of protest.

The others noticed too. "Hey, Don—wake up, dude, you're sleep-eating!" said Michaelangelo.

"I don't think so," said Splinter, starting to reach toward "Donatello." This was the final confirmation of his suspicions.

Suddenly, before any of them could say or do anything, the door burst open and Tyro dived in. A natural hunter, he had picked up the familiar Turtle scent in the storm drains and followed it back to its source in the hope of finding new friends. Now the same keen senses told him that one of the four Turtles around the table was actually an impostor sent by Krang. He raced over and sank his teeth into the robot Donatello's leg.

"Yipes! What's that? It looks like Godzilla's infant son," Michaelangelo yelled.

"Surely I'm still dreaming. That's the only explanation," said Raphael.

"Pinch yourself, bro'," said Leonardo. "That thing's bitten Don!"

"No, it has not," Splinter corrected. "Look again."

The Turtles turned to see what their master was referring to—and if they were astonished before, they were flabbergasted now.

Tyro's bite had peeled away a layer of green rubber. Now they could all see the gleam of metal from which the fake Donatello was constructed.

"A robot!" Michaelangelo screeched. "Don, you've turned into a robot! Gee, what a horrible dream!"

"It's not a dream, you dope," snapped Leonardo. He had already drawn his katana to strike, but now that the robot's true identity had been discovered it merely sat motionless and silent. Apparently its programming had been disrupted.

"What a humongous development,"

griped Raphael. "We're turned out of bed before dawn, Don turns out to be a robot, and there's a lizard the size of a bulldog running around under the kitchen table!"

"It is not a lizard." Splinter's calming voice broke into the hubbub of confusion. He extended his hand with a scrap of pepperoni, which Tyro happily took. "It seems to be a miniature tyrannosaur. And it is wearing Donatello's bandanna. How very strange."

It did not take Splinter and his pupils very long to work out the gist of what had happened. "Donatello's been turtle-napped," said Leonardo. "But maybe this midget dinosaur can lead us to him."

Tyro did not quite understand what his new friends wanted of him, but he sensed the air of agitation. After nibbling a few more pieces of pepperoni, he went back to the door and started snuffling at it.

"Attaboy, Dino," Michaelangelo said

enthusiastically. "Take us to whoever's got our bro'!"

He swung the door open and Tyro scuttled outside, running in excited circles in the sewer tunnel while the Turtles gathered their weapons.

"You follow the dinosaur, my sons," Splinter directed. "I shall remain to dismantle the robot impostor so that Krang cannot use it to cause any more harm."

The three Turtles bowed respectfully and raced off in pursuit of Tyro. They were grim-faced, and under the masks, their eyes were narrowed in menace. Whoever had abducted Donatello had made a big mistake. When you mess with one Teenage Mutant Ninja Turtle, you mess with them all. . . .

5

"Okay, dat's da last of 'em." Rocksteady added another fossil bone to the precariously balanced pile on the cart and started wheeling it back toward the mole mobile.

"Wait!" cried Bebop as they emerged from the museum that they had been robbing. "It's da Turtles!"

Led by Tyro, the three Turtles had

arrived on the scene not a moment too soon. Running at full tilt, they smashed into a trio of Foot Soldiers and sent them reeling with a succession of kicks and punches.

"Cowabunga!" Michaelangelo shouted as he laid out the last of them with a mighty punch. "Another crushing de-*feet* for the Foot."

"Maybe they'll *toe* the straight and narrow from now on," said Raphael.

"Enough wisecracks," said Leonardo, swirling his katana swords through the air. "We still have to get those two jerks, Bebop and Rocksteady."

But the mutant miscreants had not waited around once they saw the Turtles overpowering their Foot Soldiers. They abandoned the cart and started racing off toward the alleyway where their vehicle was parked.

"Quick, Rocky, head for the mole mobile," shouted Bebop. He turned to thumb his snout at the Turtles. "Haw, haw! Youse Turtles can't catch us."

"Oh, no?" Michaelangelo retorted. "Banzai!" He ran forward and jumped onto the cart, sending it careening off along the pavement after the fleeing felons. As he drew level with them, he stood up on the speeding cart and, snatching up a huge dinosaur leg bone, swung it like a baseball club. *Thunk! Clunk!* "Man, if only Casey Jones could see me now!" He whooped.

All Bebop and Rocksteady could see were stars. Michaelangelo's solid blows had put them flat on their backs. Groaning, they fingered the growing lumps on their heads and looked on miserably as Leonardo and Raphael caught up.

"All right, you misfits," Raphael said with a growl, "you're going to tell us what you've done with our brother. Like *now*, dudes!"

"Okay, okay," said Bebop, holding up his hands in surrender when it looked as if Michaelangelo was ready to administer another whack with the bone. "He's down under da ground."

"Krang's got him," clarified Rock-steady. "In da Technodrome."

Leonardo caught sight of the mole mobile beside a pile of earth and rubble nearby. Holding Bebop and Rocksteady at swordpoint, he marched them over to it. "In that case, you're going to take us to him," he said. "And no funny business." He emphasized the point by pricking Bebop's backside with the katana.

He would not really have harmed him with it, of course—but Bebop was too dim to know that. "Ouch!" he exclaimed. "We'll do whatever ya say. Just watch where ya prod dat pig-sticker, will ya?"

"It's a rhino-sticker too, dude, in case you're getting any ideas," Leonardo said to Rocksteady.

"Huh," Raphael snorted. "These bozos haven't had one idea between them in their whole worthless lives." He gave them a particularly menacing stare.

Like all bullies, Bebop and Rock-steady were cowards at heart. After a few pretend threats, they were only too ready to do exactly what the Turtles told them. After clambering into the mole mobile, they started up the engines.

Tyro jumped aboard just as Michaelangelo was swinging the hatch shut. "Excellent!" Michaelangelo cried as the mole mobile began its descent into the ground. "Krang's expecting a box of fossils, but instead he's going to get three shellsful of trouble!"

"For your sakes I hope nothing's happened to our bro'," Raphael said with a growl to Bebop and Rocksteady. "Otherwise I might just forget that you belong to endangered species."

◆

In fact, Donatello had been all but forgotten by his captors. Apart from the guard of four Foot Soldiers keeping a watchful eye on him, the other occupants of the Technodrome had their attention elsewhere.

"Those blundering manbeasts!"

Krang was ranting. "I send them to do a simple robbery, then they forget the standard procedure. They should have radioed in as soon as they had the fossils on board."

The captain of the Foot Soldiers stepped forward. "Perhaps something has gone wrong, Lord Krang," he suggested. "Shall I take a company of troops to the docking bay to await their arrival?"

Krang stared at him, pouting. "Wrong? What could go wrong? Even those bungling oafs ought to be able to steal a cartload of old bones! No, Captain—they've just forgotten, the fools."

"Probably they've got the radio tuned to an all-oboe music station," said Donatello. As the Turtle had planned, Krang only sneered and turned away at this remark. Donatello took the opportunity to sidle over to the pile of bones still waiting to be processed and added to the vat of mutagenic virus.

A bleeping from one of the control panels told Krang that the mole mobile had returned. He turned a control knob, which caused one of the overhead display screens to switch to a view of the docking bay.

"Great gargantuan galaxies!" he sputtered a moment later.

All of the Foot Soldiers turned to the screen to see what it was that had surprised their master. It was the opportunity Donatello had been hoping for. While his four guards were distracted, he stooped and started to rummage around in the pile of dinosaur bones.

"The Turtles!" Krang was screeching as he stared at the view on the screen. "They're in the Technodrome! All Foot Soldiers to the docking bay immediately!" Then he turned and noticed that Donatello was up to something. "What—?" he cried. "Grab that turtle before he does any damage!"

The four guards assigned to watch Donatello started to step forward toward him. As they did, he rose with a fossil egg that he had taken from the pile.

Pitched with a powerful overarm swing and a battle-cry of "Cowabunga!" it hit one of the Foot Soldiers smack between the eyes. He dropped in his tracks, stunned.

Donatello immediately made a feint toward one of the remaining guards, who took a step back to evade him. At the same time, the guard directly behind him reached out to grab the Turtle's neck. Donatello pulled his head back into his shell, spun around and caught the guard's sleeve while he was still off balance, and hurled him in a perfect judo throw into the Soldier who was backpedaling.

That left one Foot Soldier nearby. Donatello dropped to a crouch to avoid a sword thrust, knocked the guard's legs out from under him with a foot-sweep, and finished with a karate punch to the chin as he fell.

"Ninjutsu lesson's over, dudes," he said, dusting his hands. "Now—it's been fun, but I gotta go." And before Krang could even start to collect his wits and issue orders to the other Foot Soldiers, Donatello had darted out of the control room.

He raced along the corridor to the docking bay to find Tyro and his brothers waiting beside a mole mobile. "Hey, Don!" they cried as they caught sight of him. They were so happy to find him unharmed that they failed to notice Bebop and Rocksteady sneaking away.

"Uh-oh, scope it out, guys," said Michaelangelo, pointing to the mutant villains as they vanished up the corridor. "I'd say we've lost our pilots."

"And it couldn't have happened at a worse time!" Raphael exclaimed.

As he spoke, a whole platoon of Foot Soldiers came charging into the docking bay. Bebop and Rocksteady had reversed direction and were now leading the charge. They were a lot braver when they were backed up by dozens of Foot Soldiers.

"Gimme a blaster! Gimme a blaster!"

Bebop was saying. "I want to blow dem Turtles inta da middle of next week."

"No way," said Donatello. "That way we'd miss Thanksgiving. C'mon, dudes, let's beat a retreat!" He wrenched open the hatch of a mole mobile and jumped inside.

"But, Don, we don't know how to drive this thing," protested Leonardo, following Tyro and the other Turtles inside nonetheless.

Donatello grinned. "I think I do. Hold tight!" His first attempt to switch on the ignition just made the whole vehicle rattle like an old tin can, but he got it started on the second try. Out of the rearview porthole, they saw the snarling faces of Bebop and Rocksteady recede as the mole mobile streaked toward the surface.

On the journey back, Donatello explained all about Krang's evil plan.

"But that's terrible," Leonardo gasped. "Even though Krang didn't get the last shipment of fossils, he still has enough for one batch of the virus. If just a couple of hundred Thanksgiving turkeys turn into tyrannosaurs, think of the havoc they'll cause. Tyro here might be placid enough when he's kept fed—" he patted the tame dinosaur affectionately—"but with a whole bunch of them it'd be like having a farm full of hungry rottweilers!"

"No sweat," Donatello assured him. "During the commotion when you guys first turned up at the Technodrome, I had the chance to switch around the labels on Krang's pile of dinosaur bones. What that means is . . . well, wait and see."

◆

A couple of days later, the Turtles got a message from April on their intercom.

"Uh, guys . . ." she began. "I really don't know how to put this. I don't know if I believe it, in fact. . . ."

"Let me guess, April," Splinter said.

"There's a pack of miniature dinosaurs on the loose."

April forced a grin. "Got it in one guess. Somehow I'm not too surprised to find out you know. I'm on my way to the MacAndrews Farm at the moment, where the dinosaurs are running loose. There's a couple of camera crews on their way too, and someone has called the police and fire departments, but I don't know quite how they're going to handle the situation. Any bright ideas?"

Donatello was rummaging around in a closet. He emerged carrying four Turtle Cheapskates—the motorized skateboards he'd built for himself and his brothers. "Well, pardners, it's time to round us up some dogies," he declared.

"What?" asked Leonardo.

Raphael figured out what he had in mind. "Are you kidding, Don?" he said in disbelief. "You can't herd a pack of angry tyrannosaurs like cattle. They'd rip us to shreds!"

"*Tyrannosaurs* would," agreed Donatello. "That's why I switched Krang's ingredients. All the turkeys have been mutated into midget *brontosaurs*. They're placid, gentle creatures. And they don't even eat meat, much less bite."

"Bucking brontos!" Michaelangelo exclaimed excitedly, revving up his Cheapskate. "Bodacious!"

Sure enough, they arrived at the gates of the farm to find a milling herd of plump two-foot-long brontosaurs. Instead of the beady expression of a tyrannosaur like Tyro (who looked rather like a hawk when he was waiting to be fed), the plump little brontosaurs had large watery eyes that made them look like puppies.

First on the scene, April heard the buzz of the Cheapskates and saw the Turtles speeding up toward the farm gate. She was delighted to watch as the turtles circled the herd on their Cheapskates, and easily rounded up the slow and docile creatures.

The little dinosaurs came thundering

out through the gates, pursued by the four whooping Teenage Turtles on skateboards. Stampeding the herd toward an open manhole, they guided them down in to the very deepest areas of the storm drains. Minutes later the TV camera crew, the police, and a fire engine screeched to a halt to find . . . nothing but a quiet farm scene. April knew she had some explaining to do!

Down in the sewers, the brontosaurs seemed quite happy to slosh around in the mucky water.

"Cool concept, dude," Michaelangelo told Donatello. "They're taking to it like ducks to water."

"Even though they're really mutant turkeys," Raphael chimed in. "Look, they're feeding on the mold and algae down here."

Tyro nuzzled up to Donatello, but it was obvious to the Turtles that they couldn't keep him as a pet. Having a two-foot dinosaur around would mean too many opportunities for trouble.

"We can leave him here as a watchdog to guard the herd," suggested Leonardo. "We wouldn't want these critters wandering up onto the streets again."

"Yeah, and it's not like we're abandoning a tame pet," added Raphael. "Tyro's a wild animal, remember, and he needs his freedom."

"Don't worry, boy," Donatello said as he gave Tyro a pat on the snout. "I'll come back and visit you from time to time."

◆

"Well," said Leonardo as they headed back to the den. "We've foiled Krang's plan to turn the turkeys into carnivorous dinosaurs, and since he didn't have enough virus for more than one farm, we've managed to save Thanksgiving. But you still haven't told us how you found out about the scheme in the first place, Don."

Donatello shrugged. "Oh, you know

me. I just have this knack of sniffing out *fowl* play. *Eggs*-traordinary, isn't it?"

Raphael winced. "You know, I'm not sure I didn't prefer the robot you, Don," he said with a grin. "At least it *laid* off the rotten puns!"

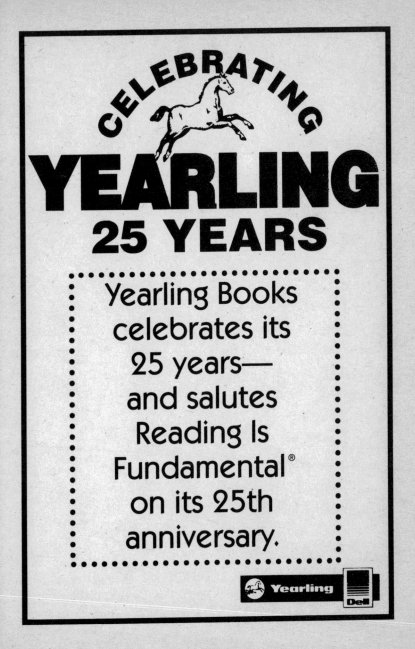